For Jerry and Nancy, my parents

BEACH LANE BOOKS
An imprint of Simon & Schuster Children's Publishing Division
1230 Avenue of the Americas, New York, New York 10020
Copyright © 2010 by Marla Frazee
BEACH LANE BOOKS is a trademark of Simon & Schuster, Inc.
For information about special discounts for bulk purchases, please contact Simon &
Schuster Special Sales at 1-866-506-1949 or business@simonandschuster.com.
The Simon & Schuster Speakers Bureau can bring authors to your live event.
For more information or to book an event, contact the Simon & Schuster Speakers
Bureau at 1-866-248-3049 or visit our website at www.simonspeakers.com.
Book design by Ann Bobco
The text for this book is set in Heatwave.
The illustrations for this book are rendered in black Prismacolor pencil and gouache
on Strathmore 2-ply cold press paper.
The display type is hand-lettered by Marla Frazee.
Manufactured in China
1110 SCP

10 9 8 7 6 5 4
Library of Congress Cataloging-in-Publication Data
Frazee, Marla.
The boss baby / Marla Frazee.—1st ed.
p. cm.
Summary: From the moment he arrives, it is obvious that the new baby is boss and he gets
whatever he wants, from drinks made-to-order around the clock to his executive gym.
ISBN 978-1-4424-0167-9 (hardcover)
[1. Babies—Fiction. 2. Humorous stories.] I. Title.
PZ7.F866Bo 2011
[E]—dc22
2009021991

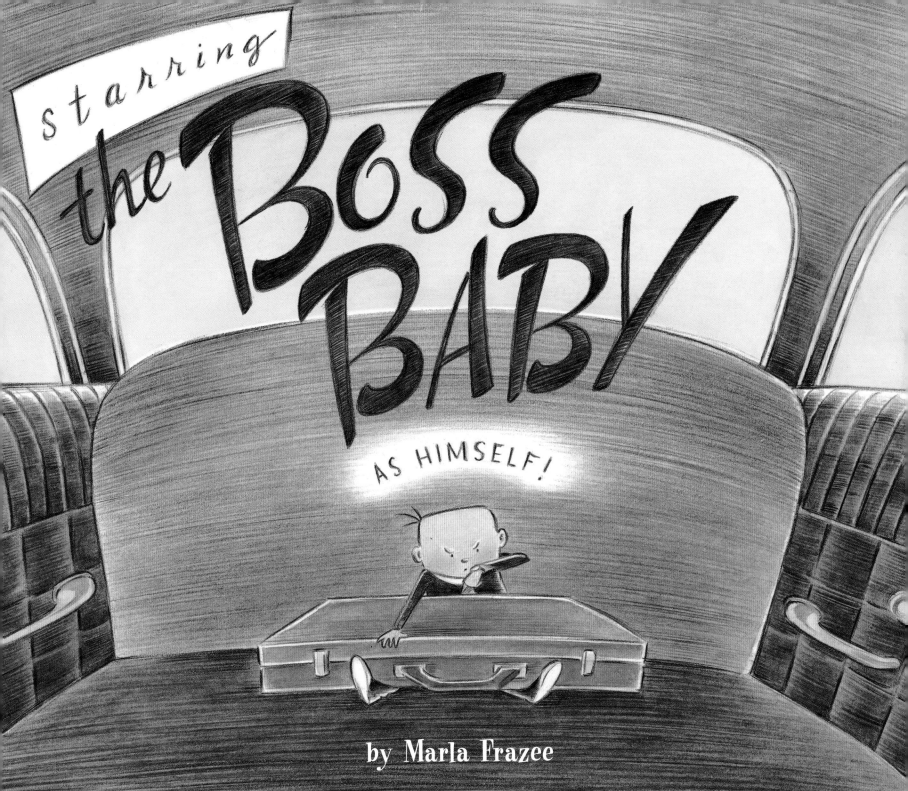

starring
the Boss
BABY

AS HIMSELF!

by Marla Frazee

BEACH LANE BOOKS   New York   London   Toronto   Sydney

From the moment the baby arrived,

it was obvious that he was the boss.

He put Mom and Dad on a round-the-clock schedule, with no time off.

And then he set up his office right smack-dab in the middle of the house.

He made demands.
Many, many demands.

And he was quite
particular.

If things
weren't done
to his immediate
satisfaction,

he had a fit.

He conducted meetings.

Lots

and lots

and *lots* of meetings,

many in the
middle of
the night.

The funky thing was, he never, ever said
a single word that made any sense at all.

But that didn't stop him.

As boss, he was entitled to plenty of perks.

There was the lounge.

The spa.

And the executive gym.

There were drinks
made to order,
24/7.

And, of course,
the private jet.

Then one day, all activity ground to a halt.

The boss surveyed his surroundings,

eyeballed his workers, and frowned.

He called a meeting.

His staff did not respond.

He called and called and called. Nothing.

The boss's usual demands were not getting their usual results.

It was time to try something
completely out of the box.

Wow. That worked.

He had to get back to the office ASAP.

There was still a business to run here.

And make no mistake . . .

he was the boss of it.